Walt Disney's

Mickey and Goofy's Race Around the World

Random House 🏠 **New York**

⊙ GROLIER
BOOK CLUB EDITION

Mickey Mouse and his friend Goofy
were living in San Francisco.

One day Mickey came walking
down the street.

Goofy ran up to meet him.

"Hi, Mickey!" called Goofy. "I have
something to tell you!"

"Look at this newspaper," said Goofy.
"A race around the world is going
to be held. It sounds just right for us!"
Mickey looked at the newspaper.

"That's not a contest," Mickey said. "Anyone can buy a plane ticket and go around the world that way."

"No!" said Goofy. "Planes can't be used in this race!"

"No planes!" said Mickey. "But how—"

"We can use your old hot-air balloon!" said Goofy.

Goofy found
Mickey's balloon
the next day.

Mickey and Goofy fixed
the balloon.
Soon it was as good
as new.

Then the friends stocked
the basket with supplies.

Soon the day came
to start the race.

A big crowd watched
Mickey and Goofy
take off.

Mickey's nephews
were there too.

Up, up went
the balloon!
"Good-bye!"
called Goofy.

What an adventure
this was going to be!

The flight across
the United States
was perfect.

Mickey and Goofy crossed over
the Grand Canyon by moonlight.

They sailed over
the Statue of Liberty
and the skyscrapers
of New York.

The balloon headed out to sea
at sunset.

During the night a storm blew up!
Mickey and Goofy hid under blankets.
The wild wind blew them along.

By morning the storm had stopped.
Mickey looked at his map carefully.
"Looks like we're going the right way,"
Mickey said. "We're over Newfoundland."
Goofy waved at some fishermen below.

For a long time
the friends saw
nothing but water.

Then they spotted
polar bears and seals
on ice floes.

"We must be close
to the North Pole!"
said Goofy.

Mickey took pictures
with his camera.

"Gosh!" said Goofy as night fell.
"Look at those whales down there!"
The wind carried the balloon
over the Atlantic Ocean.

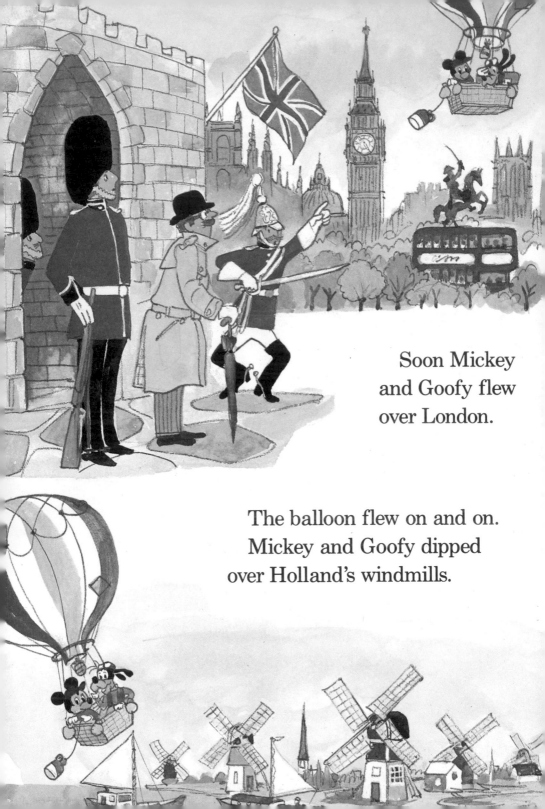

Soon Mickey
and Goofy flew
over London.

The balloon flew on and on.
Mickey and Goofy dipped
over Holland's windmills.

"We're over Germany now,"
Mickey said a little later.

The wind blew south.
Soon tall snow-tipped mountains
loomed ahead.

"We must throw out some cargo,"
Mickey said. "Or we'll hit the peaks!"
He and Goofy tossed out most
of their supplies.
But the peak ahead of them
came closer and closer.
"Watch out!" yelled Goofy.

Swoosh! The big balloon
smacked into the mountain.

The air rushed out
of the balloon.

Mickey and Goofy tumbled out
of the basket and into a snowdrift!

"Well, that's the end
of the race for us,"
Goofy said.
"No way!" said Mickey.
"We're not giving up yet!"

They turned
the basket over
and put in
the balloon
and supplies.

Mickey sat down
in the basket.
    Goofy gave it
a big push and
hopped aboard.

"Hang on tight!"
cried Goofy.
    They bounced and
bumped all the way
down the mountain.

At last the friends tumbled to a stop.
They were next to a train station!
A train was ready to leave.
Mickey and Goofy got on board
with their basket and balloon.

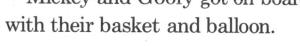

"You see!" said Mickey.
"We're on our way again!"

The little train chugged along
across the mountains.
It went through dark tunnels
and around sharp curves.

Finally the train
stopped in a town
near the sea.

A kind lady helped Mickey
and Goofy to mend the balloon.

Soon the friends
were aloft again.
They flew over Italy.
Then they crossed
the Mediterranean Sea.

"Land ho!" said Goofy after a while.
There were palm trees and sailboats.
Mickey studied his map.

"I see hills
with pointy tops,"
said Goofy.
  "Those are
pyramids. We're
over Egypt now,"
said Mickey.

The sun shone
hot and bright
above the desert.

"Look at the camel caravan!"
Goofy said.

"We must be in Arabia
now," said Mickey.
They waved good-bye
to the camel caravan.

Soon the balloon
flew over elephants!
"We must be over
India," Mickey said.

Meanwhile, two big birds had landed
on top of the balloon.
They pecked at it—and it broke!

"Oh, no!" said Goofy.
"The air is rushing
out of the balloon!"
"We're falling!"
said Mickey.

The basket fell down with a thump!
The elephants pulled apart
the balloon.

"Now what?" asked Goofy.

"We still have the basket,"
said Mickey. "We'll travel in it
across India!"

Off went Mickey and Goofy
on the elephants.

Finally they reached
a seaport.

A tramp steamer was about to set sail.

"Do you have room for us?" Mickey asked.
"Only if you can sleep on the deck," said the captain.
"Fine!" said Mickey. And off they sailed.

After a while, storm winds blew.
Mickey and Goofy huddled on the deck.
The steamer was tossed in the wind.
Then everything on deck slid overboard.
So did Mickey and Goofy!

Mickey and Goofy found their basket.
It was floating in the water.
"We can use this for a boat, Goofy,"
said Mickey. "Climb aboard!"

Goofy was able
to grab some
of the balloon
as it floated by.

Goofy made a sail from the balloon.
"Hope this works!" he said to Mickey.

The friends sailed across the ocean.
They ate fish and drank rainwater.
After many days they saw a bridge.
"We're home!" said Mickey.

The harbor in San Francisco was filled
with big ships and small boats.

They were all there to welcome Mickey
and Goofy—the winners of the race!

"Thank you for this silver cup,"
Mickey said to the mayor.

"And the check, too!" said Goofy.

"We've learned never to lose hope,"
said Mickey.

"No matter how hopeless things look!"
Goofy added.